Spiders

Written by Cherril Jones
Adapted by Dona Rice
Illustrated by Agi Palinay

Crab Spider

A spider's
not an insect.
It has eight
legs in all.

Jumping Spider

These legs are
made to take
it on floors or
up a wall.

Most spiders
sure are clever.
They spin out
silky threads.

Bolas Spider

And back
and forth they
weave them
to make their
sticky webs.

Tarantula Spider

And when the job is over, the spider waits to eat

Pirate Spider

Any insect stuck there — the perfect spider treat!

13

Zebra Spider

And if the web
gets broken
or torn in
any way,

The spider will just fix it to use another day.